THE REAL GHOSTBUSTERS

Troll Bridge

Maureen Spurgeon

CARNIVAL

Amidst the bright lights of New York City, the night clubs, the hustle and bustle, the roar of the traffic, stood a troll. His huge eyes were wide open with wonder and pleasure.

Suddenly, the sound of Break-Dance music made him prick up his strange, pointed ears, his fang teeth parted in a jagged grin. This was his chance to join in the fun!

If those break-dancers could only have seen him – twirling around, spinning on his back, dancing right through the night until the sun rose over Brooklyn Bridge. It was the start of a day like a hundred others – a broken-down truck was holding up a long line of traffic.

"Hey, buddy!" yelled a taxi driver, thumping his horn. "Get that load of junk out of here!"

   "Hey!" the man shouted again. "I said ---"
   An army of trolls was swarming in from nowhere, ripping away the roof of the truck in their great claws, wrenching off the doors, splitting open crates of vegetables. All the truck driver could do was stand back in a daze, still holding the steering wheel.
   "Holy Moses!" shrieked the cabbie. "I'm getting out of here!"
   And he wasn't the only one.
   Hundreds of trolls were swarming up Brooklyn Bridge. At first everyone sat motionless, lulled into the laziness that only a traffic jam can produce. Slowly, realisation dawned. They were not still in bed dreaming, there really were hundreds of disgusting creatures about to eat everyone on the bridge. Panic . . . as thousands of people ran to get off the bridge. Meanwhile . . .

Back at the converted Fire Station which was the Ghostbusters' H.Q. Peter Venkman dreamed he was putting his arm around this fantastic girl . . . Too bad it was his green ghostly friend, Slimer!

"Yuk!" Peter sat up, slime dripping from his arm. "Slimer got me in my sleep! Get him, Ray!"

But even a quick-thinking Ghostbuster like Ray Stantz could do nothing. Because, at that moment the fire alarm sounded and all four Ghostbusters sprang into action, ready to slide down the pole to the ground floor.

"You won't believe this," secretary Janine told them, "but trolls have taken over the Brooklyn Bridge!"

"Sounds pretty exciting!" announced Egon Spengler, eyes gleaming behind his specs. "What d'you think, Peter?"

Venkman shrugged. "It's New York. It's Monday morning. So, where else would trolls be, but under Brooklyn Bridge? Into the Ectomobile, you guys!"

"Remember the Three Billy Goats Gruff?" Ray kept saying as they raced along. "And the troll who wouldn't let them cross the bridge? Gee, this could be serious!"

"Trolls under Brooklyn Bridge!" Peter chuckled. "It's probably dogs . . . Or rats . . . Or something . . ."

Sirens wailing, ECTO 1 sped on, skidding to a standstill near a line of police barricades, a surging mass of people trying to press forward. Winston Zeddmore was the first to speak.

"Wow . . ." he breathed, his chubby face filled with alarm. "Would you look at that ---"

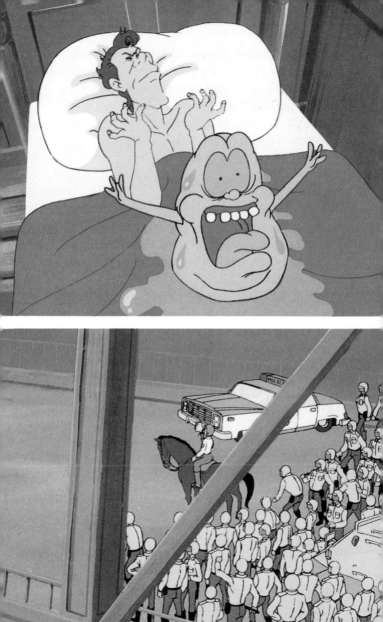

Everywhere was a sea of mangled buses, wrecked trucks and cars ripped apart, one smashed-up motor bike lay right under their noses.

"Still say it's dogs or rats, Peter?" Winston demanded. Venkman decided to ignore him.

"What's going on here, Officer?"

"Well, sir . . ." the policeman could hardly believe it, either, "these people say that trolls tore their vehicles apart ---"

Peter Venkman was quick to take charge. "Stand back, ladies and gentlemen!" he roared. "Proton Packs on, fellas! The Ghostbusters are here!"

"Ghost-bust-ers!" the crowd began to chant. "Ghost-bust-ers!"

"They're here, I can feel it," murmured Ray

Stantz, looking around for any signs of a lopsided head, fang teeth or pointed ears. "Let's drive ECTO 1 on to the bridge and see what happens!"

"Okay!" Peter gave him an impatient shove. "Get in the driving seat, and let's move!"

"Hey!" cried Stantz. "Look!" They all whirled around in their seats. "Look, you can see Brooklyn from here!"

"Never mind Brooklyn," croaked Winston Zeddmore. "Just you look straight ahead!"

As they all looked they began to feel themselves in the grip of a nightmare. Crowds of trolls seemed to be appearing from all directions, scrawny claws upraised, ready to start work on the Ectomobile! "I-I found them, didn't I?" said Stantz after a pause. "All we gotta do now is blast them!"

"No, wait," Spengler warned, staring out at the forest of troll faces. "Even if we could do it before they wreck ECTO 1, the ion-beams from our Proton Guns might turn them into stone. Either that, or they could become really dangerous!"

"Let's try talking to them!" suggested Winston Zeddmore – cowering in his seat.

"Great idea, Winston!" Venkman retorted. "Tell them I said hello!"

Winston decided to act fast. "Those in favour of Peter going out and talking to the trolls, raise their hands! That's three against you, Peter!"

Venkman was outside before he knew it.

"Me, Dr. Venkman!" he began with a nervous smile. "You – troll!"

"Grrrumph," rumbled the Head Troll. "Groo-a-lah, deemumbo-jumbo . . ."

By this time, the other three were huddled together hiding inside the Ectomobile. Slimer managed to squeeze between them to whisper in Ray's ear.

"Slimer!" Ray cried. "That's great! Hey, Peter! Slimer understands them! He can translate!"

Within seconds Slimer had zipped through the Ectomobile windscreen and was whispering hard into the Head Troll's big, hairy ear.

"Grrrumph," boomed the Head Troll again. "Dee trrroala goonah ---"

"They've lost a troll!" Ray yelled out, as soon as Slimer came back to translate. "And they want him back!"

"Then tell them we'll find him!"

"Grrump . . ." growled the Head Troll, in answer to Slimer. "Tymah-up! Zoomah, dee fure-fleegan, den zooms!"

"The Head Troll wants to send in fireflies after him, instead!" shouted Ray. "Hey, tell him we like fireflies, Slimer!"

Slimer whispered again, and the troll spun around, reaching out a giant claw towards the river.

There was the loud, rumbling noise of water gushing and churning, orange and red, fiery lights shooting upwards into the air. Then, a huge, flaming dragon rose above the river, soaring over Brooklyn

Bridge with great flaps of its enormous wings, sending giant flames falling below.

"*That's* a firefly?" shouted Venkman, feeling the top of his head. "My hair's singed already!"

"What do we say, Slimer?" gabbled Ray. "Slimer, tell me what to say!"

"Ketana!" yelled Ray, holding up his arms towards the trolls. "Nagana loywai!"

The Ghostbusters held their breath. Then, painfully slowly, the firefly dragon turned away.

"Well, that's that," said Ray when it had finally gone. "We've got twenty four hours to find that troll. After that, they'll be sending in the firefly dragons. And then," Ray let out a deep breath, "they'll level New York."

Back in the Ectomobile, the Ghostbusters began thinking hard.

"Now," said Ray, "where would I go if I was a troll? Somewhere dark and empty, maybe . . ."

"Sounds pretty likely!" Spengler agreed. "What about Holland tunnel, right under the river?"

"No." Winston Zeddmore shook his head. "Not a tunnel. If I was a troll, I'd go somewhere with excitement and bright lights, like Times Square!"

ECTO 1 screeched to a halt, and Ray and Winston piled out.

"Okay," said Peter. "You take Times Square, we'll take the tunnel. At least there won't be any fireflies down there! Proton Guns at the ready, Spengler!"

It was pretty boring at first, Peter Venkman and Egon Spengler just walked along with the traffic whizzing past them.

Then, suddenly, a large truck roared straight past them, so fast that they had to look twice to make sure they weren't mistaken.

But, yes! There was the troll, juggling fruit around with his hands and his feet, and generally having a good time!

"Get him!" yelled Egon.

"Somebody, stop that troll!" shrieked Peter, trying desperately to race after the truck. "Hey, nice troll . . . Come on . . . We've got something for you ---"

But the troll was having the time of his life riding in the truck playing with all the fruit. He didn't even see Venkman and Spengler sprinting up the tunnel behind him, and getting more and more out of breath.

Only when the traffic started slowing down did they make any progress.

"Okay," Venkman panted. "This is where we get him ---"

Too bad he hadn't noticed an ice cream van coming from the opposite direction, its tuneful chimes tinkling above the roar of the traffic. The troll pricked up his ears, his great eyes lit up, and he started jigging around to the music.

"Go!" bellowed Spengler. And they leapt on to the vegetable truck – the very same moment as the troll jumped in the direction of the chimes. Looking over the edge of the truck, all Venkman and Spengler could see was the troll dancing away on top of the ice cream van which was heading back the way they came.

"Oh, Egon," sighed Peter. "*Now*, what do we do?"

Meanwhile, Stantz and Zeddmore had been searching for the troll among the crowds in Times Square. The weather was warm for the time of year, and they both felt hot, tired and worn out by the whole troll business. An ice cream van chiming its way down the street seemed the most beautiful sight on earth.

Winston rapped his knuckles against the panel of the van, turning to speak to Stantz.

"I could do with something to cool me down," he said. "Searching for that troll is like looking for a needle in a haystack!"

The panel opened and two beady eyes peered out.

"I mean," Zeddmore continued, "the odds against us seeing that troll must be a million to one! Oh, yeah --- A strawberry whirl, please!"

As well as a strawberry whirl he was offered a chocolate flake, a vanilla fudge, a peach ripple and a toffee crumble – all held in a big, hairy claw . . .

"Thanks!" said Winston, taking the strawberry whirl and handing over the right money.

"Harrrkssh!" came a voice in response, and the hand drew back inside.

"Did you hear that?" gaped Ray, his eyes on the van as it drove away. "Harrrkssh? What sort of talk is that?"

Winston stared at Ray, then at the strawberry whirl in his hand, then Ray stared at Winston.

"Troll!" they burst out together. "Follow that ice cream van!"

But, it was no good. After hours of searching and looking around, the Ghostbusters were no nearer finding that troll, and the thought of firefly dragons reducing New York to a cinder was becoming very real. Already the city lights were coming on everywhere, with music being played in shops and arcades — just what the troll liked best.

"Whaa-hoo-hoo-hoo!" he rumbled joyfully, looking down on the bustling streets of New York. "Parrrrrrrr-ty!"

Parties were the last thing on the minds of the Ghostbusters. All they wanted was to find the troll before the twenty-four hour deadline which would signal the return of the firefly dragons. This was why they were looking down a telescope from the top of the Empire State Building.

"It's the best way of surveying the area!" Egon kept explaining. "We only have a little time left!"

"Hey, look down there, you guys! What's that behind the street band?"

"A troll!" shouted Stantz. "A troll banging dustbin lids together! Quick, let's take the elevator!"

In a matter of moments, the Ghostbusters were in the Ectomobile speeding through the streets.

Out they tumbled into the night-life of Times Square, trying to work out the best way to go.

"Hey . . ." Stantz breathed, snapping his fingers. "Music! The troll likes music! Remember? He was dancing near a band when we saw him through the telescope!"

Next minute, they were racing off in the direction of some tuneful melodies coming from a night-club.

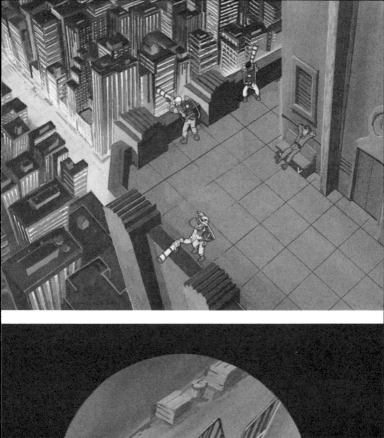

Pausing outside the door to the nightclub all they could hear was the pulsating sound of rock music. Slowly they entered. And there in the centre of the dance floor was the troll getting into the groove. Slowly they advanced on him . . .

At last, with their Proton Guns in firing position, Venkman, Stantz, Zeddmore and Spengler all jumped out together.

"You're surrounded, troll!" cried Venkman.

"Ggggrrrrr!" growled the troll, with such a mighty leap towards them that they all leapt back in fright.

"Oh, boy . . ." murmured Peter Venkman. "Where's Slimer when you need him?"

"P-a-a-r-r-r-rty?" growled the troll, hopefully, "P-a-a-r-r-rty?"

"Party?" Venkman asked the troll.

"P-a-a-r-r-rty!" nodded the troll, with a fang-like smile. "P-a-a-r-r-rty!"

Venkman grinned back and put his arm around the troll.

"Well, what d'you know? He's a party animal!"

"P-a-a-r-r-rty?" the troll pleaded, his big, brown eyes almost melting Peter Venkman's heart.

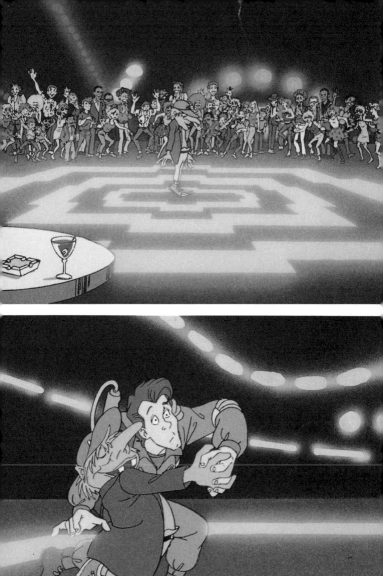

"We'd better get him back to Brooklyn Bridge," Winston put in. "Time's just about up!"

"Actually," added Egon, glancing at his watch, "our time is up."

Egon was right. At that very moment the Head Troll was gathering his army together underneath Brooklyn Bridge, all chanting together: "Fuer-fleegen . . . Fuer-fleegen . . ."

This was the sign for the enormous dragon fireflies to shoot up out of the river, swooping around the bridge in a blaze of flame and fire, fanned by their great wings. Then, one by one, they roared away towards the city, lighting up the night sky, orange and yellow and red.

The troll seemed quite contented, even though the fireflies were coming straight towards them, breathing great, scorching flames of fire. Crowds of New Yorkers were already fleeing in panic, their screams and yells floating up to Peter and his new friend.

"Hey, Egon!" Pete bawled above the roar of the fireflies. "What happens when the ion-beams from our Proton Guns hit those fireballs?"

"Don't know!" Egon shouted back helpfully.

Venkman took a chance, firing his Proton Gun and hitting the nearest firefly dragon almost by accident. But – instead of destroying the monster, it only made him more fierce and threatening than ever.

"Look out!" roared Peter, pulling the troll to the ground. "That firefly friend of yours is coming this way!"

Only just in time. Great fiery claws shot out to make a fearsome grab – but missed, completely.

"P-a-a-r-r-rty?" the troll beamed at Peter. "P-a-a-r-r-rty?"

Venkman had to smile.

The sky lit up yet again as another fireball began heading straight towards them.

"Fire!" bellowed Egon, a proton beam hitting the target.

"But there's more to come!" shouted Winston, still firing his Proton Gun as hard as he could. "What can we do?"

"We've all got to hit the same target!" Spengler yelled back. "Peter, you first!"

Venkman took aim and fired. Then Stantz. Then Spengler, then Zeddmore.

The firefly dragon stopped in its tracks. Then – POOF! Hit by the power from four ion-streams, it dissolved into a cloud of black smoke which was blown apart by the wind. The rest of the fireflies backed away in the distance.

Suddenly, it all seemed very quiet. Slowly, wearily, the Ghostbusters turned and made their way down to the street, where the Ectomobile was parked, still in one piece. Ray Stantz was the first to speak.

"They'll be back, Peter. And there'll be more of them next time, in numbers we can't cope with. There's only one way out of this, pal ---"

The troll was nestling close to Venkman, gazing at him with his huge, great eyes, soft and pleading.

"You — you don't mean he's got to go? Not my friend, the troll?"

"It's the only way," Spengler told him.

"Those fireflies will destroy the city," Zeddmore insisted.

Peter Venkman thought for a moment.

"Look," he said, "if we hit a troll with one of our ion-beams, he either gets bigger — or he turns to stone. That right, Egon?"

Venkman knew then there was only one thing to do.

The trolls were glad to have their missing brother back among them — even though he was now made of stone and tied to a trailer pulled by the Ghostbusters' Ectomobile.

"He'll be okay in about 500 hundred years," Peter told them, as they carried him away, under the bridge. "Sorry we had to blast him — he wouldn't come quietly."

All around, things seemed to be getting back to normal. Cars drove around as usual, people went about their daily business — and nowhere was there more New York noise and city bustle than the railway station, where Peter Venkman was meeting a truck with the sign "STONECUTTERS INC." painted on the side.

"Thanks again for the rush job," Venkman was saying, handing over some money to the driver. "We appreciate it!"

"Any time, Doctor Venkman!"

The truck pulled away, leaving Spengler, Zeddmore, Venkman and Stantz on the platform — along with someone in an overcoat, big floppy hat, wearing a false nose, fake glasses and phoney moustache.

"Tell him to hurry up, Slimer, or he'll miss his train!" urged Peter, and handed over a slip of paper. "Tell him to go to this address!"

"Th-a-a-ank you, Pe-te-er . . ." growled the troll, just as the train whistle sounded.

Peter was very touched. "Did you teach him that?" he asked the other Ghostbusters, but they just smiled.

"Just where are we sending him?" Zeddmore wondered.

"To a party-going friend of mine in Chicago!" Venkman grinned. "He owes me five dollars. So, once he gets a visit from our little party-loving fan, I'd call it quits — wouldn't you?"

And the Ghostbusters had to agree.

"'Bye, troll!" they all yelled, waving right back at him. "Have a good time in Chicago!"

Carnival
An imprint of the Children's Division
of the Collins Publishing Group
8 Grafton Street, London W1X 3LA

Published by Carnival 1988

ISBN: 0 00 194 438 X

Printed & bound in Great Britain by
PURNELL BOOK PRODUCTION LIMITED
A MEMBER OF BPCC plc